Julie Andrews Edwards

LITTLE BO

THE STORY OF
BONNIE BOADICEA

ILLUSTRATED BY Henry Cole

HYPERION BOOKS FOR CHILDREN
NEW YORK

Printed in the United States of America.

This book is set in Deepedene 15/23.

The artwork for each picture was prepared using oil paint on paper.

First Edition

3 5 7 9 10 8 6 4 2

Library of Congress Cataloging-in-Publication Data

Edwards, Julie, 1935–

Little Bo: The story of Bonnie Boadicea/Julie Andrews Edwards;

illustrated by Henry Cole—1st ed.

p. cm.

Summary: After being separated from her brothers and sisters, a very small cat named Bo falls in with a sailor and becomes a ship's cat, having various adventures at sea.

ISBN 0-7868-0514-5 (hc)—ISBN 0-7868-2449-2 (lib. bdg.)

1. Cats Juvenile—fiction. [1. Cats—Fiction. 2. Voyages and travels—Fiction. 3. Ships—Fiction.]

I. Cole, Henry, 1955– ill. II. Title.

PZ10.3.E254Li   1999

[Fic]—dc21   99-24797

For Amy and Jo
with all my love
— J.A.E.

To Maury
— H.C.

CONTENTS

CHAPTER ONE

The Six Kittens

ON A COLD AUTUMN EVENING, when a fierce wind bent the trees and dashed russet and copper and gold leaves into the gutters, when people retired from the raw night to sit by warm fires that hissed and spat from moisture falling through their chimneys, a beautiful white cat named Sarabande gave birth to six lovely kittens.

Sarabande was no ordinary cat. She was a champion Persian and had won many prizes. She lived with her owner, Mrs. Edith Edge, in a large house in the country, not far from the sea.

When Mrs. Edge saw the new kittens, she became hysterical.

"Look at them," she cried to her butler, Mr. Withers. "They're *all* different. Really, Withers—as I've said before, I'm very unhappy about this. And you're partially to blame. Sarabande is a purebred and a champion and she should have been treated as such. If you had kept your eye on her—as I *asked* you— then this unfortunate incident would never have occurred."

Withers gritted his teeth, but merely said, "My apologies, ma'am."

"Can you imagine what the ladies at the Cat Association would say if they knew about this?" Mrs. Edge paced the room. "Of course the kittens can't stay here. As soon as they're old enough, we'll think of something, some place we can send them. You can be sure the father is that miserable Bounder, who is always lurking around the garden." She stroked Sarabande's long, silky fur. "There, there, my precious, my beauty. We'll see to it that nasty alley cat never bothers you again. Don't you worry."

Sarabande wasn't at all worried. She was feeling very content. She thought her kittens were the prettiest in the whole world and she knew that their father, who was indeed the

infamous Bounder, would be delighted and proud if he could see his new family. She told herself that as soon as her kittens were old enough, she would take them out into the garden to meet their father.

It was not long before Sarabande's babies began to be aware of the world around them. At first their eyes were a sort of milky blue, but as the days passed, each little cat began to develop its own eye coloring and its own very definite personality.

Sarabande decided to give them each a name.

She called the eldest kitten Samson. He was the biggest of the litter and the strongest, with a thick black coat of fur. Sarabande told him he was going to be extremely handsome one day—"Just like your papa," she said proudly.

Next came Princess. Sarabande gave this kitten a grand name because she was by far the most beautiful. Like her mother, she was white, and silky-soft.

The third kitten had a sweet, contented nature. He was black, like his father, but had his mother's long fur. He ate the most of all the babies and was therefore rather fat. His mother named him, simply, Tubs.

Then there was Polly. She was shy and quiet: a small, plain cat with a gentle, sensitive personality. Her coloring was black and white and three of her paws were white—and she had a white nose.

The next-to-youngest kitten in the litter was a dashing young fellow, gray and thin and sleek. His mother named him

4

Maximillian. "Because it sounds smart and that's what you are," she told him.

Sarabande had difficulty naming the last kitten. It was a miracle that this little one had survived, for she was very, very tiny. At first it seemed she would never get enough to eat, for the other kittens were so much stronger and pushed her out of the way at feeding time. Also, there was the danger of her being squashed, especially by Tubs, who was so big and heavy and who liked to sleep on top of all the others. But small as she was, the littlest kitten had a vivacious, curious nature—and was always getting into mischief. She had soft gray Persian fur, with white ankles and paws. On her chest was a white patch of fur that was shaped like a heart. Her eyes were a perfect violet, like the coloring you sometimes see in flowers such as pansies or forget-me-nots.

This tiny creature, who almost seemed too small to be a real cat, waited for her mother to give her a name. But Sarabande could only stare at her daughter and shake her head. "For the life of me, I don't know what to call you," she said. "Your eyes are too pretty, your fur is too soft, and you are *so* small.

For the time being, you'll just have to be my little no-name baby. We'll ask your papa to think of something appropriate when he sees you."

The kittens grew rapidly. Their tails began to stand erect and their fur, still baby-soft, looked spiky and funny. Tubs's long fur gave the illusion of his being even fatter than he really was. Samson was soon able to jump up on chairs and tables, though rather clumsily at first. Maximillian began to explore the kitchen. Often he found himself far away from his mother and he would cry piteously until he found her again. Princess was mostly content to lie in one place and observe the others. She was lazy and rather vain. Sweet Polly was very shy.

Samson was the first one to start playing. The others soon copied him and they all loved it. They rolled and tumbled on the floor and pretended to fight with each other; they arched their backs and danced sideways and attacked any object that caught their fancy. They played hide-and-seek and pounced on each other and boxed each other's ears—and there were times when they would all go tearing after each other around and around the kitchen, slipping and sliding on the polished tiles, knocking things down and bumping into walls and doors and having the best time.

Withers was annoyed. "Miserable, ratty things," he grumbled. "Don't know why Mrs. Edge ever let them grow up.

I prefer dogs." He was not kind to the kittens and more than once he gave them a nasty shove with his boot. They soon learned to avoid him.

CHAPTER TWO

The Christening

WHEN THE KITTENS WERE about eight weeks old, Sarabande decided it was time for them to meet their father.

One evening, after Withers had retired early to bed, she noticed that he had left the kitchen window slightly ajar. Jumping up onto a chair and then the kitchen sink, she told the kittens to follow her.

"Wait—wait for me!" cried the little no-name kitten, for she was struggling to get up on the sink. Samson gave her a helpful shove and she was able to scramble up after the others.

Poor Tubs had a hard time getting onto the chair as he was so heavy, and when he finally reached the kitchen sink he accidentally nudged a teacup. It crashed to the floor and splintered into pieces.

Sarabande felt sure that Withers would be awakened. But, surprisingly, all remained silent. After a moment, she tapped the window with her paw until it opened a little wider. "Now, my dears, come quickly," she whispered. "You'll see the garbage cans outside. Jump onto them and then follow me to the garden shed."

It was dark, but that didn't bother the kittens. Like all cats, they could see quite well in the night.

"Now what, Mama?" Tubs asked.

"Now we wait," said Sarabande. "Maximillian, please don't go wandering off. Little One—try to keep up with us, please. Princess, pay attention. I want you all to sit quietly and behave yourselves. *This* is an important evening."

"I'm cold," said Princess in a sulky voice.

"You'll get used to it. Stay close and I'll keep you warm."

"It's a bit scary," said the smallest kitten.

The garden seemed so big and the trees and hedges cast dark shadows, their branches making a rustling sound in the night. There was the smell of damp grass and fresh wood and old leaves, and all manner of delightful scents came from the garbage cans and the nearby compost heap.

After a while, the clouds in the sky parted to reveal a large, gleaming moon, and as its light bathed the garden there was a whisper of sound.

The kittens caught a glimpse of something, some creature, black and swift. It leaped from a tree to the top of the wall, and they saw that it was a magnificent cat. He was poised, alert, proud, eyes blazing. He was unique; a handsome cat, a strong cat.

Having assured himself that all was safe, he stretched a long, lazy stretch, muscles flexing beneath his shiny fur, then sprang effortlessly and gracefully down onto the lawn.

Sarabande moved across the grass to greet him. The kittens watched, fascinated, as the two beautiful animals paused to gaze at each other, then moved forward to exchange a gentle touching of noses.

"I think Mama likes him," whispered Tubs shyly.

"Children," Sarabande called softly. "Come and meet your father."

They bounded across the grass and tumbled in a heap at Sarabande's side.

The big cat chuckled. "My, my, my! Why, they're beautiful, Sara. Simply grand. And *six* of them! Now—which one is which?"

"This is Samson," said Sarabande proudly, nudging her eldest son forward.

Instinctively, Samson tried to act like his father. He pulled himself up as tall as he possibly could in order to give a good impression and then, with easy grace, he stretched. "Hello, Papa," he said.

"—and this is Princess," Sarabande was saying.

"I'm cold," complained Princess, still sulking.

"Why, you just come and sit by me," said her father, and he put her between his front paws, where she settled comfortably. "Now, who is *this* mighty young fellow?"

"This is Tubs," Sarabande replied. "Tubs, won't you please sit up for your father?"

Tubs was so overcome that he put his head beneath his paws. "Hi, Papa," he said in a muffled voice.

"He's a little too large at the moment, but I'm afraid he's rather fond of his food," his mother explained.

Bounder chuckled again and looked at Polly.

"Hello, Papa," she said shyly. "Mama calls me Polly, and I— I'm happy that you're here."

"Why, thank you, ma'am." He bowed.

Sarabande continued, "This is our smart son, Maximillian. The other day, he got himself locked in the pantry and we couldn't find him. But he worked out how to pull down the pantry door handle and he finally got out—all by himself."

"Hey, that *is* smart," said Bounder.

Sarabande prodded the little no-name cat, who had been hiding behind her mother's fluffy tail. "I was wondering if you could help me. . . ." she began.

"What *have* we here?" asked Bounder.

The tiny, furry kitten gazed up at him with dazzling, violet-colored eyes.

"This is our youngest," replied Sarabande. "I haven't given her a name yet. She's so very small, and I simply couldn't think of anything appropriate."

"By my whiskers, you certainly are a little one," said the big cat. He leaned down and whispered in a kindly tone, "And I bet you get scared sometimes, huh?"

The kitten hung her head and nodded.

"Well, I have the perfect remedy for *that*. We're just going to have to give you a very important name: something you can hang on to when times are bad. A big, bold name helps you face the world. You can draw yourself up inside and say, "You don't scare me one bit, because my name is . . ."

"Bounder!" yelled Samson enthusiastically.

"Sshhhh," said his mother.

"Yes. Bounder is one of the good big names. Who can think of another?"

"My name's a big name," said Maximillian proudly.

"Mine's not," said Tubs.

"But *you* are," said his father. "So that makes it all right. Now, let me see . . ." He looked at the smallest kitten. "We need the perfect name . . . an outstanding name. Hmm."

The kittens waited expectantly, all eyes on the handsome black cat. He looked up toward the stars for a moment, then said thoughtfully, "When I was just a scrap, my great-granddaddy told me a tale that had been told to him by *his* great-granddaddy: about a strong and beautiful lady called"—he paused for a moment as he tried to remember—"yes, I have it. Her name was Boadicea. How about *that* for a terrific name?"

There was silence. Then Samson said, "Bodi-*who*?"

"Boadicea. She was a great warrior queen, brave and fearless, who fought her enemies and sent them away."

"But I'll never remember Bodi-what's-her-name," Tubs complained.

"All right. So we'll call her 'Bo' for short. But Bo will know that she's really Boadicea inside."

"Well, my little Bo, how about it?" Sarabande asked. "Does the name feel right?"

"I love it," said Maximillian.

16

"Me, too," added Polly.

The others agreed.

The little kitten thought about it for a moment, then nodded. She danced happily in a small circle, pleased to have a name of her own at last. She stood as tall as she could and said loudly, "I'm Boadicea!" She poked Princess in fun and received a smack on the ear for it. Everyone laughed.

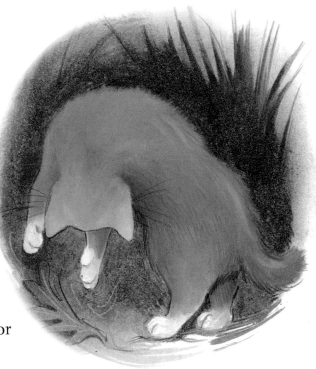

The kittens and their mother and father sat and talked long into the night.

"Where is your home, Papa? Where do you live?" asked Samson.

"Oh—I don't have a permanent base," replied Bounder. "I guess you could say the world is my home."

"Have you been to lots of places?" asked Maximillian.

"More than most cats, I reckon. Have you ever heard of Paris, France? Or Italy? I've been there. They're a long way off—across the sea."

"What's the sea?" asked Little Bo.

"Oh—that's a *big* fishpond. I'll show you some day."

"I'd love to see the world," said Samson wistfully.

"Me, too," said Maximillian.

"Me, too," echoed Bo.

"Well, you must try to do just that," said Bounder. "Don't be sit-at-home, fireside cats, like so many—"

"But I *like* sitting by the fireside," interrupted Princess.

"I can see that you do," replied her father. "But what will it get you, my pretty one? Nothing but a warm nose and a fat tummy—and that's not what life should be about. Life is for having fun, learning things, going on adventures. It keeps you on your paws." Bounder told them fascinating stories about his youth, his family, his scrapes, escapes, fights; how he could beat all the cats in the neighborhood when it came to mousing; how he had nearly been run over by a train; how he had swum a great river to rescue a little puppy; how he had met Sarabande and had instantly fallen in love with her.

The kittens listened, wide-eyed, and the dawn was almost breaking when Sarabande decided it was time to move back into the house. The kittens protested, but Bounder said, "Do as your mama says. We'll meet again soon. Careful now. Withers and I know each other well and we're not fond of each other. I don't want him giving you trouble for having been out with me." He lifted his head suddenly and sniffed. "I think we're going to have snow. Your mama will tell you what that is." He touched Sarabande's nose lovingly and nudged the kittens. "Bye, family. See you around."

He looked at the big wall for a moment, his head cocked to one side, then sprang in one easy movement to the top. With a wave of his magnificent tail he was gone.

The amazing thing was that after two days it really did begin to snow, just as he had said it would.

CHAPTER THREE

The Journey

THE KITTENS WERE SITTING at the window one morning, watching the big white flakes falling from the sky. Every tree in the garden was traced with white, and icicles were forming on the gutters of the house.

Mrs. Edge came into the kitchen. "It's time, Withers," she announced. "It's ten days before Christmas and a good moment to sell the kittens. I suggest you take them to Mr. Jones's Pet Parlor in the village and ask him to put them in his shop window. No one can resist a kitten at Christmastime."

Withers looked relieved. "Yes, ma'am. It'll be a pleasure."

"However . . ." Mrs. Edge hesitated. "I think I just have to keep *this* little one." She picked up Princess. "She is *so* like Sarabande and they will be good company for each other."

Withers sighed unhappily and said, "Yes, ma'am."

The kittens turned to each other in consternation.

"What's going to happen?"

"Where are we going?"

"Are you coming, Mama?"

Sarabande looked at them lovingly. "It's time for you to go out into the world," she said. "Mr. Jones at the pet shop will find you good homes, I'm sure. You're big enough now. In another week or so you'd find yourselves bored with this kitchen: You'd be fighting and arguing with each other. That's the way it goes."

"But *I'm* not big enough," Bo cried. "Why can't I stay with you, Mama?"

"I wish you could *all* stay. But once you have found your own homes you'll soon be happy and content. There's nothing more wonderful than belonging to a kind family who really loves you."

"Oh, Princess. You *are* lucky to be staying," said Polly.

Princess nodded. "I know it," she said gravely.

The following morning Withers got out his old bicycle and

strapped a large basket with a wooden lid onto the back of it. He lined it with old newspapers, then went looking for Samson, Tubs, Polly, Maximillian, and Bo, who were hiding in the laundry cupboard and hoping he wouldn't find them. He discovered them within minutes, and scooping them up, he took them out to the basket and dropped them in, tying a leather strap around the outside so that the kittens couldn't get out. "That should do it," he muttered. "I'll be on my way before Mrs. Edge changes her mind."

Withers pedaled his bicycle along the snow-covered roads. It was bitterly cold and the kittens were jostled and bounced about.

"He seems to be riding a long way," moaned Polly.

"It's awfully uncomfortable," Tubs complained.

Samson tried to peer through the cracks of the basket. "I don't see anything out there but a lot of white," he observed.

"I want to know what's going to happen," declared Maximillian.

"The snow looked much warmer when we were indoors." Polly shivered.

"Maybe this'll be an adventure—and fun, like Papa said," offered Bo, though she didn't sound too sure.

A half hour later the kittens felt the bicycle coming to a halt. Withers dismounted and propped it against the wall. For a few minutes all was quiet.

Then they heard Withers's voice, sounding anxious and annoyed.

"If you'd just *look* at the kittens, Mr. Jones, I'm sure you'd change your mind. They're really quite nice and well-behaved."

"I'm sure they are," said a strange voice. "But I don't want to see your kittens, Mr. Withers. I have enough kittens in my shop to last me through the New Year *and* Easter. *Everyone* has kittens to sell at Christmastime and I just cannot take another one."

Withers began to protest. "But Mrs. Edge especially asked . . ."

"Give Mrs. Edge my regards and apologies. As I said, I don't need any more cats. Your best bet, Mr. Withers, would be to ride on to Tidewater and try the vet's house there, or, failing that, take them to the pound."

"But that's twenty miles away," said Withers, shocked.

"Indeed it is. Good day to you, now."

There was a long pause; then, suddenly, a jarring crash as Withers kicked the bicycle hard. The kittens looked at each other, wide-eyed.

"Drat it!" they heard him say. "Drat the wretched animals, drat the snow, drat the pet shop." He angrily began to shove at his bicycle. "I'm not going to ride an extra twenty miles for anyone or anything. I'll tell Mrs. Edge I left them at the Pet Parlor. She'll never know."

Inside the basket, Maximillian gasped. "I don't think he's going to take us to the vet's or anywhere else."

"What do you think he is going to do?" asked Samson.

"I don't know. What is a pound?"

Bo felt her heart beating wildly and she wished she were back home, snuggling up to Mama by the big, warm fireplace.

The bicycle stopped once more. The kittens heard Withers greeting someone. He talked for a while, then said crossly, "Would you believe it, Bert? The shop wouldn't take a single cat. And I'm stuck with the lot of 'em."

The person who must have been Bert said, "Where are they, then? In the basket? Let's have a look."

Withers undid the leather strap and opened the lid. The kittens found themselves staring up at a heavyset man with a red face.

"Miserable little things, aren't they?" he said. "What're you going to do with 'em?" He pushed down the scrambling kittens with a rough hand.

"I don't know. The river maybe," replied Withers. "I'm not going to bicycle twenty miles."

"My youngsters would enjoy a cat," Bert said thoughtfully. "It's Christmas and I could persuade the wife to take one. Trouble is, these are all a bit scrawny. Except this fat one here." He grabbed Tubs by the scruff of his neck and yanked him out of the basket. "I'll take this one off your hands if you like."

"You're a pal, Bert. Thanks a lot." Withers flipped the lid back down on the basket and got on his bicycle again. "Now all I have to do is get rid of the others. Merry Christmas to you."

"Merry Christmas," replied Bert, and he walked off with the unhappy Tubs protesting and squirming in his arms.

Polly cried piteously, "That horrid man has taken Tubs. What can we do?"

Maximillian said urgently, "Something terrible is going to happen. I feel it. Did you hear Withers's voice? How evil he sounded? What is a *river*?" He was pushing at the lid of the basket as he spoke. "Samson, look! He forgot to tie this down. We must get out of here. Do you think you can push the lid so that it flips open?"

Samson tried it. "It's heavy, but I'll try."

Maximillian looked at the others. "Listen. There isn't much time. If Samson can open this basket, I'm going to climb out and get Withers's attention. You jump to the ground and run away as fast as you can."

"Where shall we run to?" asked Bo anxiously.

"Anywhere. It's better than staying with this awful man."

Polly was terrified. "How will we know where to meet afterward?"

"We won't," explained Maximillian. "We each have to run in a different direction. That will really confuse Withers and it's

28

the only chance we have of getting away. I am sure he intends to harm us. Let us say good-bye now and try to be very brave."

Samson put his shoulder to the lid of the basket. It seemed too heavy, even for him. He pushed harder, straining every muscle, and Maximillian joined him, putting his head against it.

Suddenly the lid flipped back with a loud crack. The bicycle wobbled as Withers looked over his shoulder to see what had happened.

Using his sharp claws to scramble up Withers's coat, Maximillian hung on to his collar and gave a fearful shriek in his ear.

Things happened very fast after that.

Withers yelled and let go of the handlebars to try to grab Maximillian. The bicycle hurtled toward a large tree. Samson leaped to the ground. Bo jumped and landed on top of him. Polly twisted in the air and came down hard. Maximillian flung himself clear just as the bicycle and Withers hit the tree with a tremendous crash.

"Run!" cried Maximillian.

They did as they were told. Quickly, they scattered in all directions and soon there was not a kitten to be seen; not a sign of anything except a dazed Withers holding his head in his hands and sitting by the roadside in a large mound of snow.

CHAPTER FOUR

The Escape

LITTLE BO RAN until she thought she would collapse. It was only when the wet snow began to mat her fur that she slowed a little. She was fighting for breath and her legs ached and her chest hurt. She scrambled beneath a hedge and lay there, panting and exhausted.

She wondered which way the others had gone. Were any of them hurt? Shivering, she looked out from beneath the hedge and saw nothing but snowy fields and tall trees like thin sticks against the cloudy sky.

She wondered which way she should go. The others had gone, certainly not back to the road where Withers was, so she set off, again, across the fields. But the snow was thick and deep, and she kept sinking into it.

Something caught her eye, and she saw an animal with a long, bushy tail running swiftly in her direction, its nose to the ground. Bo felt the fur stiffen on the back of her neck. Her senses told her that this was not a friendly creature, and she crouched low. It passed within inches of her, seemingly preoccupied and on the

scent of something else. Bo became aware how dangerous it was for her to be in this unknown countryside and all alone.

I have to find somewhere that is safe and warm, she told herself, and continued on.

By the time the sun went down, she was so cold that she was shaking all over. She was also starving and aware that her strength was disappearing fast.

She paused at the top of a knoll. In the distance a road stretched like a thin, dark ribbon. And far, far away there were buildings, but Bo knew she could never reach them by nightfall.

Darkness was rapidly covering the land.

She noticed some stones and planks of wood stacked against each other. Limping toward them, she saw that they were part of an old shed like the one in Mrs. Edge's garden. This would have to be her shelter for the night.

Bo crawled into the shed and found a pile of damp leaves and tattered newspapers, gathered there by years of wind and rain. She turned around and around until she had fashioned a makeshift nest for herself and, almost immediately, fell into an exhausted sleep.

CHAPTER FIVE

The Rescue

ALL NIGHT LONG the wind howled outside the shed. Bo shivered and dreamed of Mama and warm milk, and of her brothers and sisters, and of the cozy house she had recently known. She dreamed of trying to run away and of being unable to. She dreamed of Withers and of calling out for help. She slept fitfully, twitching, mewling, and shivering.

"Hello. Is anyone about?"

Bo tried to move, but she was so stiff from the cold that she couldn't even lift a paw.

"Bo. Samson. Are you near? Answer me!"

Bo slowly opened her eyes. There was an eerie light outside and someone was calling her name. Surely she was dreaming.

"Boadicea. Polly. Can anyone hear me? Halloo!"

With a great rush of joy, Bo recognized the voice of her father.

"Papa! Papa, I'm here."

In an instant the wooden planks were toppled with a crash. Bounder stood looking down at her.

"Bo, Little Bo. Thank the stars I found you."

"Oh, Papa. I thought I must be dreaming. But I cannot move, Papa."

"You must, Bo." Bounder began to lick her snow-matted fur with his rough tongue. "Get up. Stand up," he commanded. "If you stay here you will never move again."

"How did you find me, Papa?"

"I was in the village. I saw Tubs being carried by a stranger. Tubs called out to me and said he thought you had all been taken to the river. I've been searching ever since."

"Did you find the others?"

"Not yet. You're the first."

"I'm hungry, Papa. And cold."

"I know, little one. Get up now. We must get you food and shelter. Do you think you can walk?"

"I can try," she said.

"That's my Boadicea. Follow me. There's a town not too far from here."

Bounder picked his way carefully through the snow. He paused often to make sure Bo was following in his tracks.

It took an hour for them to reach the houses Bo had seen the night before. One house, older and larger than the rest, had a large collection of garbage cans near the back door.

"This is the big hotel where people come to eat," explained

Bounder. "And these cans are always good for leftover scraps." Within seconds he had found the remains of a half-eaten piece of chicken. He laid it down in front of his daughter.

"Eat," he said, and Bo needed no encouragement.

Bounder waited until the last morsel was finished. "Now, little one, listen. I must try to find Samson and Polly and Maximillian. Perhaps I can help them as I've helped you. You should be all right now. Wait until the door of the inn is open and then go inside. Lots of people live and work here and *someone* is going to have a kind heart and take care of you."

"Thank you, Papa. Will you tell Mama you found me?"

"But of course," he said warmly. "I'll tell her how brave you've been, too."

"Will we meet again?"

"I swear by my nine lives that we will," he replied. "Take care, Boadicea." He touched her nose lovingly and ran swiftly up the street and out of sight.

CHAPTER SIX

The Monster

B O SIGHED and turned her attention to the big hotel. There were delicious food smells coming from the kitchen. She sat behind the garbage cans and waited. It wasn't long before the back door opened. A man came out and dumped a large sack on top of the cans, then turned and walked back inside. Bo darted after him across the yard and stumbled up the steps. She meowed in her friendliest and most polite voice. Then she received the shock of her life.

Lying just inside the door was a huge monster. It looked up in surprise, pricked its ears, and began to growl. The fur on Bo's neck stood on end and she hissed and arched her back. The monster's lips curled back over sharp, pointed teeth, and it slowly got to its feet.

Bo stepped back, forgetting that the stairs were just behind her. She lost her footing and went rolling and tumbling down them, giving a yowl of fear.

Barking, snarling, and snapping, the monster hurled himself at the little cat. She lashed out instinctively with unfurled claws,

raking the creature's face. It yelped in pain. She raced off down the street with the animal close behind her. They dodged and weaved their way between startled, yelling people and cars, buses, and bicycles that made angry, blasting sounds. It was a miracle that someone didn't have an accident. Bo had no idea where to go. All she knew was that she had to run as fast as possible from the terrible creature who was getting closer and closer with every step.

She saw a high wall and flung herself at it.

Normally, Bo would never have been able to manage such a climb, but fear gave her special strength and she clambered and clawed her way up, up, above the dreadful, snapping teeth of the animal below. She stood at the top, looking down, breathless, wide-eyed, and trembling from her head to her paws.

The dog just could not reach her. Time and again he hurled himself at the wall. He whined and scratched and jumped and barked until he was hoarse and red-eyed and exhausted.

All afternoon Bo waited for him to go away. The dog waited, too, until suddenly it began to rain—large, splashing drops. The dog looked up to the sky, shook himself, and sneezed. After one or two last, futile lunges, he turned and ran back toward the hotel, his ears down and his tail between his legs.

Bo watched until he was out of sight. She was dazed and she, too, was wet. Now what to do? she wondered. I can't go back to the hotel, that's for sure.

She jumped with difficulty from the wall, every part of her body feeling stiff and bruised.

By now it was raining hard and the streets were almost empty. It would soon be nightfall again. A strong smell of fish came on the wind and tickled Bo's nose.

She began to walk toward this enticing aroma, keeping a sharp lookout for any other monsters that might cross her path. She turned a corner and then stopped in amazement.

Across the road, beyond piles of nets and crates and chains and coils of rope, was an enormous body of water. It was gray, with white-capped, curling waves that dashed onto a pebbly ground. Many big, floating houses were sitting in the water, rocking from side to side.

Bo suddenly realized that she was looking at the sea. It was exactly as Papa had described it, just like "some big fishpond." It seemed to go on forever. The smell of fish was everywhere, though she could not see a single one.

She huddled close to some nets, for there was no shelter. She shivered and wished with all her being that she were home with Mama and Princess.

CHAPTER SEVEN

The Young Sailor

DUSK TURNED TO NIGHT and the streetlamps came on, illuminating the gray cobblestones. Suddenly, Bo heard footsteps and someone whistling a cheerful tune. A young man appeared out of the darkness, walking toward her. He was wearing blue trousers and a big, thick jacket, with a cloth cap on his head. He paused near a lamp and turned up the collar of his coat.

Bo felt so miserable and she so longed to have someone notice her that she lifted her head and howled. She wailed—a long, miserable cry that came from her heart.

The young man looked around, startled. "What on earth . . . ?" he began.

Bo scrambled away from the nets and crawled, trembling, toward him. She heard him gasp as she collapsed at his feet.

"Good Lord, what is this?" Bo felt herself taken up by strong, gentle hands. "My goodness—whatever happened to you, little cat? It *is* a little cat, I think! What brings you out on such a miserable winter's night? You must be a long way from home."

Bo opened her violet-colored eyes and looked at the young

man. He had the kindest voice and a good face. She suddenly found herself crying and whimpering and trying her hardest to tell him all the terrible things that had happened to her in the last few days. She told him about Withers, and how she had run away, and of her long night in the snow, and how Papa had saved her and how, later, she had been attacked by a monster creature.

"Yes, yes, yes. I know, I know." The young man stroked her and held her against his coat. Bo clung to it and pushed her nose into his collar. It felt warm and soft.

"We can't stay out here or we'll both be drenched," he said. "I wonder who you belong to? Where you came from? You'd best come with me for now."

He tucked the little cat inside his jacket and walked briskly down the street. Bo sensed him turning in out of the rain, and moments later she found herself sitting on a small table in a very tiny room. It seemed that the whole place was moving from side to side. There was a slapping noise, like water sloshing around in a bucket.

The young man took off his cap and jacket and put a kettle of water on a stove to heat. He found a towel and rubbed Bo gently until she was dry and her skin was tingling. He put milk in a saucer and added warm water. He sat at the table, his chin on his hands, and watched as Bo gratefully lapped it up.

"Feels good, doesn't it, little cat?"

Bo purred, hiccuped, and licked her whiskers.

"Now, what am I going to do with you?"

Bo crawled onto his shoulder and folded herself into his neck as she had done before.

"Oh, you'd like to stay, would you?" He stroked her gently. "That might be difficult. I'm a sailor, you see, and I travel a lot; leaving tomorrow, as a matter of fact, with the first tide."

He was quiet for a moment, then took her off his shoulder and looked at her once more.

"Oh. My, my—such eyes! How could anyone not look out for

you? You're a bonnie one, I must say. If you were *my* cat, that's what I'd call you—Bonnie. But you're so tiny, I think I'd have to call you 'Bo' for short."

Bo's eyes opened wide. How could he possibly know her name?

"Oh, you like that name, huh? It does suit you." The young man smiled. "Well, now that I've found a name for you, I'd better introduce myself. Billy Bates is my name and I'm a sailor. You're in the cabin of *Red Betsy*, which is my boat. It's a herring fishing boat, and that's why it smells a bit." He was preparing a bed for Bo as he spoke. "To be honest, it's not actually *my* boat. I'm just the first mate. But I'm going to be a captain one day."

He picked up the little cat.

"I can't send you out into the rain, so you'll have to spend the night. That's fine by me. I could use the company and I don't have any family to speak of. . . ."

He placed her on a warmed blanket near the stove. "There you are, then. That's where you'll sleep. I've got to go topside now and check the lines so that we're safe in this weather. But I'll give you a good breakfast in the morning before I have to put you ashore. How does that sit with you, Bo?"

Bo licked his hand.

"I really do believe you understand everything I'm saying." Billy stroked her again. "I wish I could keep you—but our captain doesn't allow animals on the boat. Well, good night, little one. See you tomorrow, bright and early."

Bo snuggled down on the blanket. The milk had warmed her stomach and she was very sleepy. She thought about Billy Bates and how kind he was.

She was so tired, she let her eyes fall shut. The next moment she was fast asleep.

CHAPTER EIGHT

Red Betsy

BILLY WAS UP EARLY. There was a lot to be done before *Red Betsy* could set sail. His boss, Captain Svenson, was a strict man and he insisted on his sailors keeping a smart ship.

The rain had continued all night. Billy remembered the little cat and frowned. He hated the thought of having to put her ashore in such awful weather. But he couldn't keep her on the boat. Captain Svenson would never allow it. Billy wondered if one of his sailor friends in the port might look after her.

He went to get Bo, but she wasn't on the blanket where he had left her.

"Bo!" he called. "Here, little kitten. Breakfast time."

He went looking for her. He walked all around the boat, calling her name, hoping that he would find her.

"I guess she already went ashore," Billy muttered, disappointed.

"Mister Bates!"

A loud voice hailed him from the bridge. It was the captain. "The tide isn't going to wait. At this rate we'll not get back until

Christmas. On the double now. Get the lads moving. Cast off and come topside."

"Aye, Captain." Billy began his chores, all the while keeping a lookout for the little gray cat. He checked with some of his shipmates.

"Have you seen a tiny cat—about *this* big?"

But the answer was always, "No, Billy. Sorry."

Bo had vanished, and Billy could only hope that, wherever she was, she was warm and safe.

There was a flurry of activity. Ropes slapped the deck, the engine throbbed, the fishing tackle shifted and creaked. *Red Betsy* weighed anchor, her chains screaming, and slowly she pulled away from the shore. It was a blustery day, and once past the harbor wall, Captain Svenson increased speed and the tough little fishing boat butted into the big, swelling waves.

"Right, Billy," said the captain. "I've set a course. I'm going below for some coffee. Keep an eye on things."

"Aye, sir," replied Billy.

He sat in the captain's chair and looked at the sea and thought about Bo. He was fond of cats and there were always lots of strays in the harbor that needed a bite of food.

But he had never seen one as pretty or as tiny as the kitten he had found last night in the rain. He wished he had been able to say good-bye to her.

"MISTER BATES!"

Billy sighed. Whenever Captain Svenson was angry he called him *Mister* Bates. Something was definitely wrong.

He ran to the captain's cabin.

"Yes, Captain?"

Captain Svenson was pointing at his bunk. "Would you mind explaining *that*?"

Billy gasped. Bo was lying in the middle of the bunk, purring and blinking her lovely violet eyes.

"There you are!" cried Billy in a pleased voice. He picked her up. "I thought you'd gone ashore."

Bo licked his chin happily.

"Captain, sir—I'm sorry about this. She's a stray I found in the rain and I was going to put her ashore this morning."

"Well, we're not turning back, Mister Bates. What do you suggest we do?" the captain asked testily as he scratched his neck.

"I'll be responsible for her, sir. Could I keep her with me, until we get back to port, that is?"

Captain Svenson looked at Bo. "I don't like cats. I especially don't like them on my boat. They make me itch! One hint of trouble and she goes overboard. Just see she doesn't get in my way."

"Right, sir. Thank you, sir."

Billy went topside and set Bo on one of the big coil lines.

"I'm glad to see you again," he said, stroking her.

Bo purred. She was glad to see Billy, too.

"Well, I guess you're going to have to be a ship's cat for a while," declared Billy. "But you'll have to learn about boats and the ways of the sea. And you'll have to avoid the captain. Do you think you can do that?"

Of course she could. With Billy Bates looking out for her, Bo

felt she could do anything. She was very happy. She looked out
at the gray water and enjoyed the feeling of the boat riding up
and down over the swelling waves. This was the beginning
of an adventure. Wouldn't Papa be pleased if he knew?
Billy stood on the deck, the wind ruffling his hair,
and Bo sat proudly beside him.

CHAPTER NINE

Troubles

DAYS PASSED AND BO BEGAN to learn all about the life that went on aboard *Red Betsy*.

The boat was a fishing trawler, a tough, tubby, cheerful-looking vessel, built to endure heavy seas and bad weather. She was high in the prow, which enabled her to cut through rough waters easily, and on her aft deck was a strong winch with a block and tackle, nets, and other gear: everything that a well-equipped fishing boat would need to get the fishing done.

Besides Billy and Captain Svenson, there were five men on board: Charlie, Kim, Bryan, Jack, and a cook, affectionately known as Muffin. They were a hard and willing crew and worked as an efficient team.

At first, Billy kept Bo safely in his cabin, for he didn't want the little kitten wandering around and getting lost, or possibly falling overboard. But at least twice a day he took her topside—which meant that he took her up onto the main deck for some fresh air and exercise, giving her the chance to meet his friends and to play.

Everyone loved Bo and made a great fuss over her—everyone, that is, except Captain Svenson.

The first time that Bo went on deck, she wasn't sure if she would like it at all.

There was a stiff breeze blowing and *Red Betsy* was plowing into the waves, rising and dipping as if in rhythm with the big engines throbbing below. Billy set Bo down, and immediately the cold wind blew her long fur in all directions. She flattened her ears. A spray of saltwater doused her and, as she shook herself in disgust, she almost fell over. It was hard to keep her balance. She held her tail high, stiffened her legs, and danced along on the tips of her paws.

Billy laughed. "Relax, Bo. You look like you're made of wires. Move with the boat and feel how she goes. You'll soon get your sea legs."

62

He picked her up and walked with her to the stern where she saw the churning water, white with foam, and the wake stretching far into the distance.

Bo sniffed. The air had an interesting smell: a combination of damp seaweed and the fumes from *Red Betsy*'s funnel, and there was that marvelous fishy odor coming from a huge pile of nets stacked nearby. She shivered as the wind gusted again.

"Sorry, Bo—it must be cold out here for such a little thing as you." Billy opened the top of his jacket and folded it around her so that only her head was exposed. He rubbed her velvety chin. "Glorious, isn't it? Nothing else for miles and miles. It's like the world belongs to us. And look at that red sky. We'll have fair weather tomorrow."

Bo soon got used to going topside and, as Billy predicted, she quickly found her sea legs. The more she adjusted to life on board, the more Billy allowed her freedom. Within a week she had found many comfortable, weatherproof "observation posts" from where she could watch all the activities of the fishing boat.

The crew were kept very busy; *Red Betsy* was full of noise and movement: always creaking, groaning, her strong wooden beams adjusting to the pounding sea and the weather. She had a ship's clock with a bell that rang in a delightful clear tone every fifteen minutes, day or night, and a horn that gave Bo a terrible fright when she first heard it—a deep, blaring bellow, harsh and discordant, that seemed to rumble up from the heart of the boat.

When Billy was alone on the bridge, Bo sat with him, and she would watch the big ship's wheel swinging, first one way, then the other, thumping gently as it adjusted to the pressure from wind and water and the set of the rudder.

There was a machine that Billy called "sonar." It made a unique pinging sound when it was turned on and somehow it was

able to tell Billy when *Red Betsy* was close to a lot of fish.

Best of all, Bo liked it when it was raining, for then Billy turned on the ship's big window wipers and they swished and sloshed, back and forth, in a comforting way.

One day, feeling particularly mischievous, she sprang at the wipers, but of course they were on the outside of the glass. Bo danced along the inside, leaping high and then crouching low trying to catch them, making Billy laugh so hard that he was unable to prevent what happened next.

Bo nudged his large mug of afternoon tea and upset its contents all over the sea charts and papers that were strewn across the console, just as Captain Svenson returned to the bridge.

He saw the brown liquid spreading across his precious maps, and roared his disapproval.

"MISTER BATES!"

Startled, Bo leaped onto the captain's chair and streaked off down the companionway.

"Oh sir, *sorry*, sir." Billy hastily tried to wipe up the tea with his sleeve, then his kerchief. But it simply made things worse.

"That dratted cat! That mangy, miserable ratty piece of tat!" The captain began to scratch himself violently and his face became red. "You'll buy me new charts, Mister Bates, and I'll thank you to remember what I said: Keep that furball out of my sight!"

"Yes, Cap'n. Absolutely." Billy was ashen.

The incident was not mentioned again, except by his crewmates, who teased him mercilessly.

One day a vast shoal of herring was spotted and the sea was luminous with them. The huge net had been let out into the churning water. The cables of the winch strained to draw the heavy load toward the boat, then lift it out of the sea.

The white seabirds hovered in the air, squawking and jostling each other, hoping to snatch a morsel.

Bo watched in amazement as the big net, full to bursting with wriggling, shimmering fish, was slowly hoisted up and maneuvered over the deck, depositing great showers of water and seaweed. It hung for a moment above a large open hatch, and just as the boat leveled, it let loose a cascade; a brilliant silvery slithering stream of fish that tumbled out of the net and into the hold.

Captain Svenson yelled, "Clear the lines! Close the cargo hatch! Look lively!"

Bo was mesmerized by all those wonderful creatures that had been lifted so miraculously out of the sea.

Where had they all been until now? Papa had said it was a big fishpond, but he had never hinted at how many fish would be in it. How she wished that he or Samson or Maximillian or Tubs could be with her now.

A few of the herring had escaped the net and were flip-flopping about the deck. Bo left her observation post and crawled forward on her belly; then, steadying herself against the motion of the boat, she sprang in a mighty leap on one of the beautiful, unsuspecting fish. It thrashed and slid away from her. Bo experienced a wicked thrill and went after it, sniffing at it gingerly and tapping at it with her paws.

She got it between her teeth and was just about to run back

to her corner when a large hand picked her up by the scruff of the neck and shook her until her bones rattled. She dropped the fish, twisting and turning in alarm, and found herself staring into the purple face of Captain Svenson.

"MISTER Bates!"

"Sir!" Billy came running, sensing trouble.

"I want this wretched piece of fluff off my deck and out of the way." He tossed Bo as if she were a rag doll. Billy caught her deftly.

"I've warned you about this, Mister Bates. I don't want that cat spoiling good fish and costing me money. I don't want it around. I'll thank you to keep it locked up from now on."

"Aye, Cap'n."

Billy sighed and took Bo to his cabin.

"Grumpy old salt," he muttered under his breath. "I'm better at his job than he is and he knows it. Well, Bo, we'll just have to be more careful."

From that day on, Bo was confined to Billy's cabin whenever the heavy fishing work was being done. Sometimes she was there

for long hours, and she hated being away from the action. She could hear her friends moving about on the deck above and Captain Svenson shouting orders. There were intriguing screeches and slapping noises and thuds. She knew she was missing a lot of fun and wished she could be with Billy and all those glorious fish.

But always the cabin door was tightly shut, though she tried and tried to open it. Bo had to content herself with gazing through the porthole at the gray-green sea and the gulls, and the huge waves that dashed against the glass and made everything blurry until the water swirled away.

CHAPTER TEN

The Storm

ONE DAY WHEN IT WAS windy and cold, Bo was allowed a rare moment on deck. She stayed in a dry corner behind a life jacket—as far away from Captain Svenson as possible. She watched Billy working with the nets and wondered when he was going to give her something to eat. The fresh air always made her hungry. She could see a lot of white foam out on the lead-gray water, and the sky was dark and angry-looking.

Billy called, "Bonnie! Here, Bo," and she ran to his side. He picked her up and said to the sailors, "Batten everything down good and tight, lads. Have your weather gear ready. We're going to need it. There's a storm coming. A big one, too. Force Eight, I'd say."

Bo had no idea what "Force Eight" was, but she sensed that something was about to happen, for as soon as she had eaten her meal, Billy put her on his bunk and said, "No more going topside today, Bo. Too dangerous. Be a good girl. I'll be back." He took his yellow raincoat and hat from the back of the door and got out his thick black waterproof boots. Bo knew with a sinking heart that she was going to be shut in the cabin again and she made a dash for the companionway. Billy stuck out his foot and she tumbled over it. He scooped her up, laughing.

"No, little one. This is the best place for you today, believe me. You wouldn't want to be anywhere else." He went out and closed the door firmly behind him.

Bo jumped down and sniffed at the bottom of the door, then worked her claws on the wooden floor, tearing at it in her annoyance. She got back on the bunk and looked through the porthole. It was raining and the boat was pitching and tossing more than usual. Eventually she settled down, resignedly, and tried to sleep.

Billy, meanwhile, had joined Captain Svenson on the bridge. It was hot and stuffy there, for the doors had been closed and made watertight. The window wipers were busily hissing back and forth. *Red Betsy* was being assaulted by heavy rain and strong winds, but she bravely tackled the enormous waves, lifting high up out of the water, then thudding down hard again, her stern occasionally clearing the sea altogether and showing the powerful, whirling propellers.

"Nasty bit of weather, Billy," the captain was saying. "This hit us faster than I thought and we're in the teeth of it. I hope we don't run afoul of anything. Check the radar!"

Billy steadied himself and looked into the miraculous machine that traced any other ships or rocks or objects in the vicinity. It was hard to keep his balance. As well as plunging and rearing,

Red Betsy was slewing from side to side and both he and the captain had to hold on tightly to avoid being thrown about.

"Lord—it's a storm to raise the shipwrecks!" exclaimed the captain. "I'm going to ease the helm, otherwise we'll broach. I wish we were nearer the coast. We could have made a run for it."

"This must be a Force Nine, Captain," Billy said as *Red Betsy* swung violently over, then righted herself after what seemed like an eternity.

"At least," replied the captain as he spun the wheel. "We're taking on far too much water."

Billy thought about Bo and hoped she was all right.

Bo was far from all right. She was being thrown about the cabin, and although she dug her claws into anything she could hang on to, it didn't do much good. She went sliding this way and that, meowing in alarm as she collided with the furniture. She wondered what she could do to get out of the way of the moving objects.

Red Betsy's sharp prow plunged into a towering wave. Her timbers shuddered as she strove to heave herself out of the water and be free of its tremendous weight. For long seconds it seemed that she would continue on down into the depths, then slowly, painfully, she rose up, water streaming off her sides.

There was a loud *crack*, and on the bridge Captain Svenson spun around.

"That's the winch, Billy!" he yelled. "The rigging must be broken. Quick! Get a couple of the lads and see what you can do. The whole aft deck could be taken out."

Billy yelled for Charlie and Bryan to join him and flung open the door. Immediately the screaming wind and rain tore at his clothing.

"Keep one hand for yourself, lad," cried the captain, turning the wheel this way and that in order to keep the boat as steady as he could.

Billy and his friends made their way carefully along the side of the boat, holding on tightly to anything they could grasp and pausing every now and then as a wave of water engulfed them.

Slowly but surely they clambered to the aft deck.

The winch arm had indeed broken free and was swinging wildly from side to side, pitching up and down like a horse, and the heavy chains that had held it secure were free and whipping in the gale.

Charlie reached up to catch a chain that was passing close by. *Red Betsy* heeled over suddenly and he fell to the deck. The next moment he was washed across the boat by the dashing sea.

"MAN OVERBOARD!"

Billy heard the desperate shout and saw his friend slipping past him, his arms outstretched in panic. Charlie's body hit the rail hard, and for one second the force of the water pinned him there.

Billy flung himself forward and grasped Charlie's fingers just as the boat righted. He prayed silently and hung on with all his strength. As *Red Betsy* rolled again, he dug his heels against the bulwark and flung out his other arm, encircling Charlie's shoulders. Slowly, he dragged him aboard again.

The two men lay exhausted and gasping. Charlie could not speak, but gratitude showed in his eyes. Then his expression

turned to horror as he pointed in panic over Billy's head.

Another huge wave was upon them and the two men clung to the rigging as it smashed onto the boat, which was slewing around like a cork in an emptying bathtub.

A seething, boiling mass of water raced across the decks and tore open the hatch that covered the below-decks companionway. Gallons and gallons of water poured down the steps and pressed on toward the door of Billy's cabin.

Bo heard a loud thump. The door burst open and the water crashed into the cabin and dumped itself all over her.

She cried out in fright and spluttered and coughed. Then,

seeing that the door was open, she wasted no time in scrabbling frantically for the steps, through the swirling water.

Up, up she went and came flying out of the hatch half crazed with fear. She was assaulted by the stinging rain, and an icy wind tore at her fur.

She looked desperately for Billy and saw him just as he was getting to his feet. She also saw the loose chain and the big wooden block swinging wildly out of control and heading directly toward him.

She did not see Captain Svenson, who, having left the wheel in Kim's capable hands, was carefully making his way toward them. His foot came down hard on Bo's tail.

She released all the pent-up emotions of the last hour in a tremendous shriek of pain.

The captain yelled and fell with a thud. Billy turned and saw the swinging block only inches away from him. He ducked—just in time for it to pass viciously but harmlessly over his head.

Captain Svenson and Bo rolled over and over as *Red Betsy* wallowed in the heavy seas. Water engulfed them and pulled Bo to the rail. She fought to gain a foothold as the runoff dragged at her little body. Some frantic strength helped her make headway and she rushed straight into Billy's arms.

Bryan was helping the irate captain to his feet. He was bellowing orders and gesticulating wildly.

"Get the hatch closed! Tie down those lines! Throw the cat overboard! Move, lads!"

Billy had no choice but to act quickly.

He shoved Bo down the companionway and slammed the hatch shut over her head.

She rolled and tumbled down the stairs, dazed, bruised and half filled with water. Blindly, she raced back to Billy's damp cabin, jumped onto the bunk, and retreated into the farthest corner. She gazed wide-eyed at the door, which was swinging open and shut, expecting another body of water to come hurtling through at any moment. It didn't, though cups and plates and other loose items were swilling about in the wash on the floor. She was shaking violently and her tail was aching horribly. This

fishpond was not a good place to be today. She curled herself
painfully into a ball and began to lick herself dry.

CHAPTER ELEVEN

Bo and Billy

CAPTAIN SVENSON HAD A ROUGH TIME guiding *Red Betsy* through the storm, but eventually the worst was behind them and, within an hour, they were in calmer seas.

The captain was in a black mood and his hip and foot hurt where he had fallen. He glared at Billy.

"MISTER Bates. We'll be heading for port; the winch will need attending to. And that cat of yours—it has to go."

Billy experienced a sinking feeling in his stomach.

"Cap'n, I can't tell you how sorry I am for what happened. I had Bo locked up. With all respect, sir—and I'm sorry you hurt yourself—but if she hadn't caught my attention I would have been knocked overboard for sure. In a way she saved my life."

"Well, she nearly *killed* me," replied the captain testily. "I'm disappointed in you, Billy. You pick up a stray and allow yourself to get all sentimental about it. We'd be Noah's Ark if I allowed all the lads to bring an animal on board."

"This was an exception, sir. I certainly didn't *intend* that Bo stay with us."

"Well, she's bad luck. I want her out of the way."

Billy looked miserable.

"I can't do that, sir.

"You can't or you won't?"

Billy swallowed, then looked directly at Captain Svenson and said, "I can't and I won't, sir."

"Very well. There's not room for all of us. I suggest you leave the moment we get to port. You're fired, Mister Bates. Take your precious cat and find a job elsewhere. That's final."

Billy went below. It was indeed a miserable day.

Bo was delighted to see him. She crawled into his lap and he examined her to make sure there were no bones broken.

"Are you okay, little one?" Billy asked, as he stroked her gently. "I'm sorry I had to be so rough with you earlier, but it was all I could do." He held her up and gazed into her face. "What have you done to me, gorgeous? I've never stood up for anyone as I did for you today. And now I'm out of a job and we're both in a pickle. What do we do?"

Bo licked his nose, and all of a sudden Billy felt better and began to chuckle.

"You know what, Bo? You could be the best thing that ever happened to me. Who wants to be stuck on a herring boat all his life? There's no future in it and besides, old Svenson has been bothering me for too long."

He got up and began picking things up off the floor.

"What we're going to do is to start having some *fun*, Bo. That's what life should be about." Bo thought Billy sounded just like Papa.

He pulled out a big duffel bag and began stuffing his belongings into it.

"We'll go off and see the world," he continued. "It's what I've always wanted to do. We'll see it together, Bo. I don't care what the captain thinks—I *know* you saved my life today. You're my lucky mascot, that's for sure. We're a team, little cat, and tomorrow we'll see what adventures we can find."

Bo watched Billy and thought it all sounded grand. She felt so happy she began to purr.

She wished she could tell Mama that she had been right; there *was* a glorious feeling belonging to someone kind and loving. By some miracle she had found that someone. As far as Bo was concerned, she'd be content for Billy to do anything or go anywhere he wanted—just as long as she could be by his side.

JULIE ANDREWS EDWARDS is one of the most recognized figures in the world of entertainment. An exceptional vocalist, actress, and humanitarian, she is perhaps best known for her performances in *Mary Poppins*, *The Sound of Music*, and *Victor, Victoria*. Her television show *The Julie Andrews Hour* received eight Emmy Awards, and she was critically acclaimed for her stunning performances on Broadway in *My Fair Lady* and *Camelot*.

She also loves to write, and this is her third children's book.

HENRY COLE is a master at creating whimsical original characters. His many celebrated children's books include *Livingstone Mouse* by Pamela Duncan Edwards, *Moosetache* by Margie Palatini, and his own *Jack's Garden*.

Adept at observing the natural world, Mr. Cole brings a unique perspective to his work as an illustrator.